MATTHEW BALLEZA

Year of Plenty

Copyright © 2022 by Matthew Balleza

All rights reserved. No part of this publication may be reproduced, stored or transmitted in any form or by any means, electronic, mechanical, photocopying, recording, scanning, or otherwise without written permission from the publisher. It is illegal to copy this book, post it to a website, or distribute it by any other means without permission.

First edition

*This book was professionally typeset on Reedsy.
Find out more at reedsy.com*

To all the friends who listened to this the first time, in the gold room...

Year of Plenty

"It's amazing what a little makeup can do; how a little dark around the eyes and rouge around the lips can make a woman a Woman, can spook the plainness and tameness out of a shy girl- give her an edge, make her jump out at you. I like a woman with an edge. Always have and believe I always will. I get that from my daddy. He chose my mother way back when she was a hot mess of a woman, that's what he says. Way back when she was skinny as a toothpick and fiery as a match. He says that too. Said she had the reddest head of hair on two legs. Well, something must of happened if that's the case. Either she lost her edge, or had too much of it, or not enough of the kind he wanted, because after 30 years of wedded *something*, (I don't say bliss cuz it wasn't that) he left her. He moved three neighborhoods down from our house in Glen Burnie, Maryland, and has been there ever since. It was never well said why it happened or what caused it, but I guess when they told us we must have half expected it, because it didn't come as a shock. My sister and I were away much of the time too; me in my own little world, she in hers. And Ellie..."

I wrote that passage not long after high school, years ago. The box I pulled it from was in my mother's attic, which has a rickety set of stairs that unfolds to the main floor. She doesn't go up anymore. She sends me. Today she sent me climbing to retrieve her something- I don't remember what, because I got sidetracked. When I poked my head through, I tugged the string light, and this box was the first thing illumined; it was unmarked, sitting by the ledge of the attic door, aside from the others- the flaps were folded onto each other incorrectly, the sides dented, and by the estimate of my handling, the contents were sparse and wanted filling. I had the sense that the box sought me, not the other way, and it looked lonely somehow, if that's possible for a box to look. It looked as if it awaited a final say, a final word on its belongings. I spun it on the floor for a clue, before undoing the single strip of filmy brown tape holding the top. Through the gap I peeked in, recognizing as I pulled it open, my own handwriting on wide ruled paper- a pile of pages stacked in a disheveled spirit. The first passage began as I quoted above. I remembered writing it. Back then, I would ascend the attic on nights I couldn't fall asleep, and try to put memories down on paper to help me get back to sleep. It never worked that way- I ended up more awake than when I started, and I ended up writing about the same four people all the time: Mom, Daddy, Clara (my sister), and Ellie. The story of one of them is the story of all of them. But Ellie I owed the most words to, and still do, and it was her story that found its way to the top of the stack. Seated on the splintery floor under the bright burning bulb, I read and read, and the more I did the more I regretted where the story went, and how little I knew back then. I had left it standing; it needed catching up to pace. Thus, stealing the old manuscript, abandoning my original errand, I descended the rickets eager to retell:

Back in high school- we went to the same high school, Glen Burnie High- Ellie and I ran track and field together. She was tall and fast, and coach always got on her because she never tied her shoes right. They always came undone in the middle of the race. She was a middle and long distance runner, I was short; the first time I knew I liked her was when I saw her running the 1500m at some meet, and she's way out ahead, when her shoelace comes undone, and coach sees it and yells, and she sees it too, but she tosses her hands up and keeps running. There was no stopping her. She actually won that race. I thought 'what a run, what a free spirit'. Man, she could run and run, and I loved watching her run, loved watching her kick at the end and outchase the field, even girls that were faster than her. She was all heart all the time. She had a ponytail that would do this dancing bob when she sprinted. Back then I sort of looked like her. Our hair, at least. We both had long hair, and I was a skinny white kid with a crooked nose. That much hasn't changed. The first time we met was after a fall track practice (our senior year). The guys had done a run around the neighborhood, the girls were on the track, and when we finished, they had finished too, and she was sitting on the grass untying her shoes and zipping off her track pants. I remember that her hair was down and partly covering her face, and when I got closer I could see that there were little bits of broken leaves in her hair. I said 'Hey' and she looked up, and I said 'I'm Jonah.'

"Ajonah, you said?"

"No, sorry, just Jonah."

"Oh ok, sorry, I'm Ellie." We shook hands.

"Good to meet you, Ellie. You're fast out there."

"Well thank you. I have to run, actually; not here, I have to go now, but I'll see you at practice."

"Bye."

She was flustered by her own pun, which was cute. The next day she nodded at me at practice, the day after that I nodded at her, and that's how we began to acknowledge one another. I was shy, and didn't want to just go up to her again and start talking. I liked those little nods we shared, that little moment when I'd said hello. But I inquired, too. Some of the guys on the team said they knew her.

"Ellie Beards." I'd say.

"Beards is her last name?"

"Yeah."

"That's hilarious." one guy began,

"She doesn't really do anything." another said.

"What do you mean?"

"Like, I haven't seen her at parties. She hasn't hooked up with anyone, or at least anyone that I know. She stays at home I bet."

"How do you know?"

"I don't. She just looks like she does."

Those were the kind of speculative conversations I'd have with guys on the team, and they always let me down. No one knew anything, and anything they did know about a person, especially a girl, was revealed so crassly that it made everyone sound scummy, like people were puddles, nothing more. Anyway, when I saw Ellie it was different. When I saw her, I felt mystery, plain and simple. If she was plain at all, or simple at all, she was plainly-mysterious and simply-mysterious to me. Whatever shrinks might say about the over-sexed mind of a 17 yr. old, when she was before my eyes, I felt something very different. Attracted? Yes. Nervous? Yes. But also *shifted*. There was a shift, a fault line shift. I stood near something great and dangerous. She was like a new kind of *gravity*. It was weird. My nagging desire to speak with her made me more unlikely to open my mouth at all. I didn't want to rupture anything, our small back and forths. But that didn't last. One day after practice I asked her out. Something came over me. I had been thinking about it all day in class and it was killing me. I asked her if she wanted to go get ice cream. She was sitting down on the grass (I always seemed to ask her something when she was sitting down). She said 'When?' I said 'Now?'. Then she stood up and for the first time looked me straight in the eyes- and Good Lord were her eyes green! My goodness. Bright green, green as moss. Maybe it was the sun hitting them just right, but I had never seen eyes like it. I searched the ground, nervous. 'Sure.' she said. And when she said that, I admit I was very surprised. What a day! One minute I'm scratching my head in math class thinking when I'm going to see her, what I'm going to say to her if I do, the next I'm loading her backpack and duffle in my family's old Toyota Camry and driving five minutes down the road to The Custard House. On the way there she did her hair, which was like this small feminine ritual that kept us from talking right away. I remember it. I remember her sitting on the ledge of her seat, tossing her hair in front of her, taking one of her hair ties off her wrist and putting it up in a tight ponytail. Then readjusting and readjusting. I had never seen a girl do that in my car before and I kind of liked it. When she finished we were there.

At the custard shop I ordered vanilla-chocolate swirl with rainbow sprinkles and she got the same thing but without sprinkles.

I said, "No sprinkles?"

She said 'I'm not a sprinkles gal.' and smiled.

"What kind of girl are you then?"

"Don't know. she said, licking her cone. "I'm not a sprinkles gal though. I know that much."

It was nice to talk to her, for the first time really; to be there in that chilly, empty, middle of the day custard shop, sitting on stools in our red and white loose fitting tracksuits. I remember seeing my partial reflection through the glass window we were sitting in front of, and thinking how greasy and unkempt I looked, and wondering 'how in the hell did she decide, on such short notice, to come along with a kid like me, to get- not even ice cream, but custard?' I learned her father was a dentist, Dr. Beards of Glen Burnie, her mother stayed at home; she had two older sisters who went to the community college, and two younger brothers in elementary school who collected artificial fish bait that they played with in their rooms. I asked her if she had any nicknames and she told me she got the nickname "Ellie Elms" from her dad, because she loved elms and trees in general. When she told me that, I thought of that first time I met her, when there were leaves in her hair, and that I had better keep my mouth shut, but she saw I had a thought and asked me what was it.

I said 'Nothing. I just remembered something.'

She licked her cone and said 'Remembered what? Tell me!' Then she tapped the butt of her cone on my hand to get me to confess and I guess that's all it took to pick my locks.

I said 'It was the first time I said hi to you.'

"You mean when you caught me by surprise?"

"I did? I definitely wasn't trying to."

"Yes, you did, but what were you going to say?"

I paused. I probably blushed.

"You had leaves in your hair."

"Leaves? I did?"

Her cheeks reddened.

"Yeah." I said.

She looked away from me, out the window, and touched the end of her ponytail; this tiny, almost involuntary gesture of self consciousness.

"I kind of liked it actually." I added.

She turned all a sudden and said "You liked it? Why?" She said it with gusto, with a sly grin on her face. I'd never seen her so animated before; it was nice. It was nice to hold some pleasant secret that she sought.

"I thought it looked pretty." I said.

She got quiet. Licked her cone. The quiet was unnerving. I licked my cone too. I second guessed if I said something foolish, but that wasn't what my tongue felt, or my heart. The tongue felt right. The comment was right. I had never used a phrase like that seriously and sincerely in my whole life. And now I did. Also, I liked how it came out of my mouth, the very sound of the words, the meaning of them.

"That's very sweet of you, Jonah." she said softly. Right after, she put the palm of her hand to her temple and gave me a happy frowning look.

"I got a headache." she said.

"A brain freeze?"

"I think just a regular headache."

"Do you get those?"

"Yeah, pretty often."

"What from?"

"I never drink enough water."

We both laughed. I got her some water and she sipped it and both our custards melted away while we sat. Inside I swooned. I was the melted custard. She said "What about you? Nicknames?"

I said "Bird-dog."

"Bird-dog? Who gave you that one?"

"My dad."

"Why?"

"He says because I'm ugly when I run."

We traded weird stories like that. Bits and pieces of our weirdness. I relished it. I relished the weirdness. Each other's weirdness; those critical details that made us more substantial to each other. In one conversation too! Life was sweet, life was so sweet. I desired in that moment that life would dilate from there on out; expanding like a giant set of lungs, and inhaling the endless breath of all that was good, all that made the heart, soul, and body skip.

I drove Ellie back to the high school and she got out; but before she closed the door, she peeked in and said 'Thank you, Jonah. That was nice. See you at practice!' then winked at me. She winked! It needs repeating. She. Winked. Girls don't wink. Girls weren't supposed to wink. I was supposed to wink! My mouth fell ajar. 'She winked' I kept thinking as I drove away. What does that mean? What was she trying to tell me? I sighed the whole way home. I sighed heavily, audibly. I enjoyed sighing. It was my new sound.

From that point, Ellie Beards became my diet. Day and night I thought of her, and more and more I wanted to be next to her; talking to her, anything with her, at all times if I could. I liked how quick things moved, and I think she liked the same. On the weekends we got up early and ran through the waterfront neighborhoods in Annapolis; the streets were windy and wet; the houses were a hodgepodge of ages and styles, like the neighbors themselves; some were old brick, having been there forever, from the first days of settlement, others were new, boxy and charmless; the kind built in the 70's. But they shared in common the pale nautical colors that were iconic of the town; navies and whites, greys, muted yellows and greens. It was an area that, in its architecture and appearance, eschewed the look of brightness and ostentation, and reflected a kind of well-lived-in shabbiness; it was a shabbiness offset by the sight of water, made intimate by water. Sometimes we'd go the morning after a rainstorm and the streets would be sleek and gleaming; puddles, reflections, here and there, and what I remember so well was the sound of her running beside me; the soft quick squeak, the form of her in my periphery, even then, this crazy beautiful feeling of being with someone; with a girl. Whenever we ran downtown, we'd stop at the docks, look out for a while, smile, and keep going. Her ears and nose got red when it got cold; her whole face had a clean, salt sprayed, wind flushed look to it. Her eyes? Absurd. They were so green. When we ran fast her eyes would tear up and run down her cheeks and I would tease her that she was crying. Her hair got feathery and wispy. It was the hair of a girl who knew what briskness was, who was up for anything. I could feel that just by the way she ran beside me. When we'd finish we'd eat hot Vietnamese noodles and drink hot tea nearby. That was our day. It was so simple; I miss that. On the weekdays Ellie would come over to our house for dinner. She had a big appetite for a skinny track and field girl, and she also ate anything that my mother put before her, which impressed my mother greatly. Later on in the evening, when Ellie had left, my mother would pull me aside and say that that was a good trait in a woman, that she had a good appetite. And I'd ask why and my mother would say because you'll eat anything too. And when a girl eats like that, and is still skinny like that, it means she's doing things. I could see the logic in that. Sometimes after dinner Ellie and I would go up to the park near my house. I'd lend her one of my big coats and a beanie, and we'd walk out into the navy blue darkness and hold hands on the swing. We wouldn't swing very high but just kick off the ground a bit, finding our enjoyment in that nippy air and tiny bit of motion between us. One time it was dark enough that I couldn't really even see her, but I said, 'I want to be with you.' And she said 'I want to be with you too.' When she said that I got so nervous that I just wanted to get up and do something or go somewhere. Those words; they were too big and too much for me. Sensing all my fidgetiness coming from my swing she said 'What is it? What's gotten into you?' And my first thought was YOU! but I said,

"Nothing. I just want to do something."

She chuckled.

"Like what?"

"I don't know."

"Don't you like this enough? Swingin' next to me?"

"Yeah, I do."

"Well then?"

"Well what?"

"I mean Jonah, I don't get why we gotta do anything but be

here with each other."

I huffed.

"I don't either." I said.

"Boys," she said.

"Boys what?"

"Boys nothin. I don't know a lick about em.'"

"You know me."

"Yeah, a tad."

"And same with you." I said.

"Mhmm."

Right then and there I leaned over on that aimless frigid October evening and kissed her on the cheek, swing to swing. Her cheek was cold, but I tell you what; that moment there was the finest that life had to offer in my opinion, and not many have topped it since.

She was the first girl I took to a party, Ellie Beards. A few days before the party I told her she should wear some makeup, and she said 'Why should I?' I said because I knew the other girls would be, and I think it'd look nice. Don't your sisters have some?

'Sure they do,' she said, 'but first, who said other girls are wearing makeup, and second, you've never asked me that before.' She had a skeptical look on her face; eyes fixed, pursed lips, arms crossed. In truth, I'm not sure why I asked her to make herself up- maybe because I hadn't been to a big party ever, and now that Ellie and I were together I wanted to be enviable, or showy. Possibly it was just that I felt that I could ask more of her and she would do it. I knew she would. She'd be up for anything. The evening of this party I pick her up from her house in my daddy's Dodge ram. This thing is nice, real sweet: red on the outside, leather on the inside, great stereo, the works. When I arrive at her house I get out and watch her walk down from the stairs wearing mini heels, jeans, a tight black tee and dark brown leather jacket. She's got her hair down and her face done up all dusky; she looked like a different girl altogether. I was nervous looking at her, and I think she was nervous being looked at, walking down those stairs toward the car. I looked different too. I had scrubbed up, put on a button down, dark jeans (not sweats for once), boots. Come to think of it, we matched pretty well and hadn't even planned it. I gave her a hug, and stepped back to look at her again, and she goes,

"What?"

"What do you mean 'what'?" I say

She shakes her head "No, nothing."

We walk on. Then we stop again; I stop us.

"All good?" I ask, looking at her intently, trying to see if I misunderstood something.

"Yeah." she says.

"Really?" I ask.

"Well, do you like my outfit?"

"Yeah, pretty good." I say loosely; not believing that's the real cause of her hesitance. And as I look her closer in the face I see this chunk of mascara sitting on her eyelash, and without even asking I reach over and try to get it, but she ducks away, saying,

"What? Stop, what are you doing?"

"You got something there, in your eye."

"In my eye?"

"On your eye, on your eyelash. I wanna get it." and I reach again to get it but she pulls away again.

"How bout you just tell me and not try to fix it yourself."

"Hey, what happened? What came over you?"

"I'm wondering the same thing. I dressed up for you, Jonah. But you seem underwhelmed or not impressed or irritated or something. I can't tell which."

"Well, I'm not any of those." But the words were so weak rolling off my tongue.

How does autopilot work? I want to know. How is it that words so far from what we want to say or intend to say come pouncing and tearing out of our mouths to make a mess from nothing. When I saw Ellie that evening, I thought she looked beautiful. That's what every bone in me said, but somehow what comes out of me is this timid voice, this 'Pretty good', this bloodless compliment! It doesn't even count as a compliment. It's a non phrase, a nothing of speech. God. Where does that come from? And why did I choose to keep unraveling that hem when I could have reversed, and simply said 'Sorry Ellie. Let me start again. You're the loveliest thing standing under the stars tonight. By you, everything else looks dark and made of shadow. I'm the lucky fool who gets to call you my date. How can that be? Don't answer that. Just tell me you're ready and we'll go.' But those words never came. She fixed her makeup and we got in the car and drove away and she looked out the window most of the time. When I asked if she was excited to go she nodded, but nothing more.

The party was alright. It was trashy, more like it. They threw it in a barn. Lots of people from school came. A thousand empty beer cars littered the floor. The lacrosse bros drank the most. They were in a wild show to outdrink each other, and the more they drank the more their faces became bloated and red, and when they were really wasted, even cherubic, like little drunk boy-men trying to impress the girls who came, and who actually seemed to be impressed by the drinking. Some of the girls drank a lot and they stopped looking like girls. Ellie did not. She stayed athwart and marveled at the mess. The beer smell ascended from the ground, strong and steamy; cheap obviously, and the October air was cutting through the barn doors. People were urinating behind the barn. They'd come back in, still zipping. Ellie and I hung in separate corners for a while. She was in the corner near the pong tables; I stood near the main doors. The air was freezing, and I wasn't engaged in any particularly good conversation, but for whatever reason, I stayed put and let that air cut me in the back, right through my shirt. When I got too cold, I'd take a few steps in, into the swelter of bodies and yelling, perspire a little, then retreat back to the doors, sip my beer slowly, and let that sharp air stick its teeth into my back again. I drank enough that evening. Eventually I lost Ellie too. I lost sight of her while I was swaying. I could feel myself swaying. I looked around and didn't see her, but I couldn't move so well. Eventually she came up to me and sturdied me with a strong hand and looked at me with those crazy green eyes of hers.

"You ready to go?" she asked.

"Think so." I said. I think I said that.

"Are you alright to drive?"

"I believe so." That's what I said, a perfect lie.

So we got on our way to the car, parked on the road, and as we did she linked her arm through mine and let me lean myself against her. I wasn't all gone. And I wasn't all there. But I trusted in her arm and remember keeping my head down while we walked through the cold, ankle high, wet-looking grass, making footprints in it. Looking back, that handicapped stroll was the most intimate thing we did that evening, and I'm glad I had her to hold me up. She had mercy on me that evening. She could tell I wasn't so hot after the party. I languished through and through, and when I looked at my face in the rearview mirror it scared me. No color whatsoever except the red rim around my eyes and the dark of my eyebrows, the rest was pale. When were buckled in she said 'Alright, let's go to 7-11.' 'What for?' I said. She said 'I'm hungry and so are you.' and I said 'How'd you know?' and she slapped me on the thigh, looked straight ahead and said, 'Intuition.' I couldn't argue with that, so I turned on the car and drove with a heavy foot, hanging face, and a fearless helpful beautiful girl beside me to 7-11. When we arrived, she got out of the running car while I sat there parked and shut my eyes. When I opened my eyes she had two beef patties, one in each hand. She took a bite from one and handed me the other. Actually, I grabbed the other. I tried to. But she pulled it away and said 'Wait!' then broke it like a loaf, gave me one half, then she took the other, and we raised our halves, cheers'd nothing, and ate. I chewed mine like a cow, I remember that. I heard myself sighing and huffing after every bite. At one point she asked,

"How are you feeling, Jonah?" and I responded with

"Hey, have we kissed?" I laughed out loud; a tipsy, syrupy kind of laugh, if that makes sense.

"No...well, you've kissed me on the cheek."

"Yeah, but that doesn't count."

"Yes it does!"

"Then why'd you say no just now?"

"I changed my mind I guess."

"Then let's try another." I said.

"You want to?" she said reluctantly. I knew she was reluctant, given the swings of the evening. Perhaps my sole persuasion came by my suggesting something romantic, something that could have sweetened the night.

I said "I feel fine. Here, try."

With that, I shut my eyes, more out of tiredness than passion, slouched over to her side, still strapped in my seatbelt, tried to undo it, but couldn't- so she pushed it for me and I almost fell on top of her, opened my mouth. I had never kissed a girl before. I figured you just opened your mouth and let it happen. That's what I knew. The rest should come, right? I knew she didn't know better either. She followed my lead and did the same. So our open mouths met and I could smell the food in our breaths and I heard a clicking noise and clumsily pushed off her arm rest, which I was leaning on, to check what it was, and she said

"That's the blinker."

"How'd that happen?"

"I think you bumped it when you came over here." I shrugged my shoulders and leaned over to kiss her again but she turned her cheek and I kissed that instead.

"Hey!" I said humorously. "Hey, I'm playing."

"I know." she said "I'm just tired." She looked resigned too. I drove her back after that, made sure she got into her house ok. She waved. I drove off, grumbling through the sleepy suburbs in the big red truck.

An American boy feels a strange power to drive alone through his hometown in his father's truck; which smells like his father, with the stereo at his command, beer in his belly, and a smooth-

confused, tender tipsiness in his brain, and a girl who's far too much for him in every way, suddenly heavy in his heart. Traffic lights are more than traffic lights on nights like these. Roads in the dark go off forever, to the ends of the world; specks of headlights coming from the other way- other cars and other folks thinking the same things as you. You're cruising and the radio is soft (I play it softer the later it gets), the tune seems inevitable; a soft pop ballad you haven't heard in a long long time, and there's a hill in the road that you accelerate down, then coast; your stomach turns a notch- which is a good roller coastery feeling- You come at last to some stop lights, or blinking lights, and to pause all a sudden is to feel your blood and thoughts and whatever else is haunting you that night come out. You can't help but think of the evening past; what went right and what went wrong; the feeling of love, the hunger for more and more and more of it (if that was it). To drive at night in the suburbs, in my father's truck; that's another one of those things I've never gotten over. Don't believe I ever will.

When I returned home that night, I slept on a blanket on the hardwood floor of my room. Pulled a pillow from my bed and laid there with all those thoughts within me. The ground felt good that night. I can't tell why, it just felt so, so good. But after that night, something happened between Ellie and I. We saw each other with less frequency. When we did spend time together, we were both on edge. We seemed to get bored faster. We could no longer sit idly any more and be content. We had to move, we had to be onto something else. It was early spring of our senior year. Around this time she began to mention that she was going to be going away to college soon. I didn't want to hear that. I didn't want to think or talk about that at all.

One day we were sitting by the docks in downtown Annapolis and I was fed up with our small talk and this protracted season of quietness, so I asked "Where are you thinking of going?", dreading any response.

"JMU." she said.

"James Madison?"

"Yeah."

"That's a hike from here."

"I know, but I like the school and I've been talking with their track coach."

"You could run for them?"

"I hope so."

"You still want to run?"

She was quiet and brought her knees up to her chest on the bench.

"If you want to say something, say it please!" she said, staring ahead. She'd never raised her voice like that before. I looked at her. Her eyes were red and wet. I should have rubbed her back, told her it was going to be ok; any small bridge, but I didn't. I clasped my hands together and put them between my knees, like I was prepping to crush something between my palms. I continued,

"I meant run FOR school. Run AT school. James Madison, on their team."

"I know, I know. I know what you meant." she said. "I just, I just couldn't help myself the way you said it."

We were both quiet. Then she asked,

"You got any idea where you want to go?"

"I'm probably sticking around here at the community college for right now. We can't afford a big school anyway, I don't think. Then again I haven't really talked to my parents about that."

"Why not?"

I shrugged. "They've got their own stuff they're going through."

Looking out over the water, sitting next to Ellie that late afternoon; side by side, but not close; sparely touching; our hands tucked in our own pockets, our arms unlinked; each to each on that uncomfortable metal bench, preserving our individual warmnesses. We shared only the view. The day was overcast and the water reflected it. It reflected, too, an unkind vision of the future, grey and opaque. There were so many unspoken thoughts between us, that went out with our stares to the water. Maybe, in truth, we were in the water already. Her with the boat, the oars, the rudder. Me with the raft, held together with twine, thudding back to shore. Every time I saw Ellie after, I felt like I was puppeted by the great grey hand of the Unknown & Unspoken. It blanketed every setting, every mood. My delight in her resisted delight. My liberty with her resisted liberty. I did not marvel at the way she ran on the track, or ran beside me on our weekend runs, though we still did those. All was common. All was slag. Plain, plain. At the same time my parents had begun their talk of splitting up. I was no dummy. I heard them, though they wanted it to be confidential and private. That sort of thing never stays private, not for long. My sister was away in New York already and had no gauge. For my parents, it was never the violent outburst in the home that scared me, but the sad noises of bodies moving aimlessly through the house after dinner. I wanted to see anger. Anger was at least proof of life, proof of caring for something, or rebelling against something...But silence, silence. My poor mother. Steadiest of all of us. I felt for her the most, as much as I could, in my own numb, sympathetic-son sort of way. I absorbed her weariness too, just by being close to her. When she did laundry I'd sit in the room over, not far. When she made coffee, I'd sit at the table next to her and look at old pennysaver ads. My mind sought out mindless things like that. My daddy would come in - who could forget the sound of that front door? the blinds clacking against it when it opened - and sit down and eat the dinner that mother prepared. Dutifully and solemnly, he ate. Dreadfully solemn. Each of us looking past one another or down at their plate - mom still filling our glasses with water- not a single 'thank you' or acknowledgement from daddy or myself; what a shame - just the sound of the pitcher filling the glass - I loathed that sound. I loathed a lot of sounds then: the incidental sounds of eating there at that mini table where we sat so close together and could hear each others breathing and swallowing and forking and coughing. I felt that we were all suppressing the sound of our eating, so that we didn't bother each other, but I'm sure it had the opposite effect. Carried through every meal was my own deep sense of panic. At times I wanted to overturn the table just to get an expression, a regular expression, a human reaction on someone's face; something inflamed or catch some brightness or darkness in their eyes that proved that we were living still.

I see and think all this looking back. I confess I never did what would have taken a courageous amount of bone headedness to do, and actually flip the table. I went my own way after dinner. So did my daddy. So did my mother. We stonewalled each other. My daddy out of spite, my mother out of sadness, myself out of lonesomeness. I went to bed early those days. All I wanted to do was sleep. I went to bed listening to the sound of plates being put away. That was March. March was still frigid like the winter. My hair was down past my shoulders at that point. I remember that. Another month, another inch. Ellie was still around. In reaction to all that was painful in my family life, I clutched her closer. Despite our present tension, she was the one person I felt I could depend on. Each day at home made me want her more. I wanted to get past the empty conversation. I wanted to change her mind about going away. I wanted to give her something to miss. She was mine, after all.

One day after practice, her name and mine came up in the locker room. Someone asked "Who runs the girls 1500m on our team?" Someone else said "Ellie Beards." Then someone else said "Right, Jonah?"

I said, "Yeah, that's right."

One of those guys, I forget his name, added "You're with her, aren't you?

"Yeah."

"How are things?"

"With her? Good, but it'll be hard when she leaves."

He made a jesting, mocking laugh.

"Come on!" he said. "When she leaves? Ha! That's not the issue. Make sure she comes back."

"What do you mean?" I asked.

I really didn't know what he meant, or if he was being insensitive.

"Come on. You know what I mean. Don't bitch about it...GET IN HER PANTS!"

The other guys laughed. Then that guy, whatever his name was, came closer to me and offered his advice:

"Tell her you love her. Ok? That's number one, always works. Two, tell her you can't ever be without her. Say something like that. Get creative. Finally, and this is the most important part, get in her fucking pants!" He really enjoyed those last words. Then he explained,

"That's how girls work. They're emotional, they need to be assured you care- so show 'em' you care, say your piece, then they're yours, they're like open textbooks. They'll want to come back, trust me. Just make sure they don't cling."

Then he shoved me in the chest, nodded, and laughed again with the other guys. Abrasive as he was, I took his words to be my guide. They were the only guide I had at that time, and I was hungry for anything that could work.

That wasn't the first time for either of us. We hadn't kissed before we met, that's true, but we both did stuff our sophomore year that didn't need kissing. That day we were in her parent's house, in the basement. A movie flickered in the background; the volume low enough that I couldn't hear, but apparently she could. She seemed more interested in the movie than me. Her face suggested boredom, sustained boredom. When we were done, I felt powerless, spent. A stinking saliva taste in my mouth. I dressed quick, and she lay there. I covered her with a blanket. The credits were rolling. The basement smelled of lounging bodies. I hadn't noticed it before. I was tired too. Sullen. Irritated. Hungry. I remember I was wearing a hand me down shirt from my daddy with a little hole in front, which I never took off that whole time. Ellie sat there looking ahead, just like that time when we were looking out at the water, but this time more lazy-eyed, like her eye wasn't holding onto any one thing; she kind of turned slowly to me and said lethargically,

"You didn't even kiss me."

I don't know if that was true, but I felt scorned either way and said,

"Yes I did."

"No. You didn't."

So I kissed her on the cheek, and her expression didn't change. I said I was going home. She didn't move, or bat an eye, or even say goodbye. So I left. I figured I'd done what I needed to do, and now she'd come back. When I drove home I kept the radio off. My finger found that little tear in my daddy's old shirt and I pulled on that hole the whole way home, till it was gaping. When I looked down at it, it half amused me, half sickened me. My mother saw it later and said 'What happened to your shirt?'

I said 'It got a hole. This shirt is old anyway.

"It wasn't like that before."

"Whatever…" I said.

After that episode, it appeared that the trick worked, mostly. She came around. Ellie and I did everything normally again, it seemed; running, dinner at each other's houses, wasting time on weekends. But she was altered, too. There was a new urgency I felt in her; an urgency in being with me, an earnestness to learn who I was, even though I thought she knew almost everything. I was as plain as they came; she knew about my family already. My mother gardened, my father was an airline pilot. I had no secrets I said. 'I have no secrets.' but she looked at me skeptically. 'You've got more to you, Jonah.' she'd say. And I'd respond, 'Maybe you know something I don't then.' That conversation happened multiple times. She took interest in me. But, to be fully honest, I did not take that sort of active curiosity in her. My craving to know more about her; the details of her life, how her favorite color changed over time, or the time she cracked her tooth during a swim meet- the kinds of stories that poured out of her incessantly- stopped. It halted. I had little to no motivation answering her- and even when I was prompted to dig deeper, I had no good answer. I swung at nothing. One time she asked me,

"Have you spun in a field before?"

I scoffed.

"I mean it. Have you?" she said.

"Probably once."

"You should do it again sometime."

"Maybe. Maybe not. What made you think of that anyway?"

'Maybe' was my go-to answer. 'Maybe' was my dodge. I avoided all hypothetical questions that required an unreal commitment. I had had enough. I was sated with Ellie Beards. That line kills me, but I can't erase it.

In the middle of rereading this part of the story, I stopped and put the pages down. On a separate page I wrote her something, out of plot-

Ellie, It's odd to address you directly, here and now; in the middle of a story I know so well (and so one-sided); but I can't help thinking of you. Your voice helps. I can hear you. I wonder why I write sometimes. Why the night holds me like it does. It's as if you were conjured by my writing it; all of you, flesh and blood; smile that I first remember. And in my addressing you, I want to try to depict you as you were to me back then (faultless, true), and are still now. I was not like you. You know that. I was a hollow and starving boy. Though I've become less so. My hope in writing is that I would come to understand more fully the working of your powers in my life. How you were who you were. How you are who you are. If I've been changed at all for the better by your influence, you should be the first to know.

Then I put that sheet aside resumed the story-

Ellie came over one afternoon in April and helped dress our house for my mother's surprise birthday party. She brought scissors, streamers, tinsel, tape. The house was glamorous when we were done. My mother, who had never had a surprise party thrown for her, was so surprised that she shrieked for a full ear-popping minute. Many guests came and the party was a huge success. Ellie stayed around and helped serve. She ladled meatballs out of the slow cooker; the word 'ladling' even captures the spirit of it. It has a servanthood in it, a poverty. It makes me think of simple meals. Soups. Well, I saw that in her that night. I saw how happy she was to serve. And being as I was back then, I became bitter. I came around to the kitchen. I said you don't need to be doing that anymore, why are you still doing that? People can get their own, you don't need to do that. She looked at me with such fierce, clear, steady eyes, let the ladle sink into the slow cooker, and let me pull her into the living room. When guests began to leave, I said we should go out too, I'm getting claustrophobic. We packed her party supplies in a grocery bag and left. It was a chilly spring evening. We drove around Annapolis, down by the water, didn't really talk much. I needed to drive more than she did. I had my window all the way down, she had hers up. I took her back home and parked in front. "Jonah?" she said softly.

I turned to her.

"Are you ok?"

"What do you mean?"

"With everything going on right now? With you? your family, me leaving soon, us?

I felt my teeth clench.

I said to her,

"So, you're leaving me?"

"I'm not leaving you. But I am leaving for college. We've talked about this. I've told you a dozen times, you just ignore me though.

"I'm not ignoring." I said. "I just don't know what to say."

"You don't have to say anything."

She took my arm and held it. I was tense. A voice in my head whispered 'You don't like her anymore', and when I looked down at her head resting on my shoulder, I believed the voice. I took my arm away. She was hurt by that. She folded her arms, leaned aside, and shut her eyes. I shut mine too. We both sat there, not sleeping, not nothing, just breathing; breathing takes its own strength sometimes. Breathing in duress. Minutes passed. More minutes passed. She began to doze; as she did I grew angrier and angrier. Her tenderness, which I had just dismissed, I now wanted. I demanded. I didn't want her dozing against the car door. I wanted her tangled in MY arms, on MY body, inquiring into MY thoughts, asking of MY troubles, being troubled over MY troubles. But she slept. Her hair was kept in a loose ponytail and it fell over the front side of her shoulder. Two inches stuck out from the hair tie. The white grocery bag was between our seats, and unhesitatingly I opened it, took the small scissors and cut off an inch of her hair. It didn't cut all the way through with one swipe. I had to snip, snip, snip. I caught most of it in my hand. Then I threw the chunk out the window and looked back at her still sleeping. I let out this brief, unplanned sob all of a sudden looking at her, then dried my eyes when I heard her waking. She turned to me,

"What is it Jonah?" She asked groggily.

I avoided her face. I couldn't see what my own eyes looked like, but I knew they were bloodshot. She said I'll let you go and she one last time caressed my arm then unbuckled and smoothed her ponytail behind her and stepped out toward the house. There was so much pent-up, unarticulated fury in me I could break my hand against a wall. I thought of her that night when I left. I pictured her groping her way to her room in the dark house, and falling asleep without the least idea of what I'd done, then waking to find out for herself; finding stray pieces of hair on her clothes, and wondering How? Then the thought of me doing it, followed by her quick rejection of that thought ('Jonah wouldn't do that.' No he wouldn't. Would he?) That thought would itch, would swell. She would connect the dots, I knew. It was a mess, I was a mess, and I hadn't the backbone to tell her anything. In school I avoided her as much as I could. But one day she found me after lunch and pulled me aside.

"How could you? How could you?"

I was not ready for her. A little boy like me was not ready for those search-light eyes and stricken face.

"How could you?!"

"I'm sorry. I didn't…"

"Do it?!" she said.

"No, I did. I mean, I didn't…mean to."

Even to my own corrupted self I could not reconcile those statements. She kept looking into me, finding out the truth without my saying it.

"Jonah," she sighed. "Jonah…I can't do this right now. I'm leaving for school. I've been so troubled for you, and by you lately. Maybe I've been some of the cause of that.

27

I was dead quiet.

"We can talk again, ok?" she said. "But not for a while."

"I'm sorry…I…" but I couldn't finish the sentence.

She looked beyond me now at the traffic of bodies coming down the hallway after lunch, flowing past us. She looked at them like she was looking into a rush of moving water, reading to plunge off the sinking stone on which she stood.

"I know, Jonah." she said lastly. Then she plunged.

Just like that she was gone. I told my parents that evening, and it was the first thing I said in a long time that looked like it joined their hearts in sympathy. They were crushed for me. And I was crushed by their being crushed by me. It was hard for me to be weak for them, in general, but especially now. How could I bare my wound without telling more of the story, more of what I'd done? I feared that the weight of such shame would sink us all, and we were already sinking. A month later, my daddy moved to his new place down the street. Ellie moved off to college. I began two summer classes at the community college, and worked part time at a putt-putt course nearby. I lived with my mother. Life was happening. There was never a plateau of reflection to rest on. Nothing stayed, nothing rested in my life. However, the activity was good for me. The classes. The unskilled summer job. The longer days. Clara came back for a week, and during that week I lived vicariously through her stories of New York. She was full of energy, full of the music of the city, and it was contagious. I caught some of it. I made some friends at putt-putt; two in particular, brothers named Stephen and Pret Dexter. Pret was short for Preston, but we called him Pret. They were two lazy white kids like me who both went to community college. At dusk, when the driving range officially closed, me and the Dexters would put on tall rubber boots, tie strings to golf ball buckets, and cast them into the artificial pond and drag out golf balls by the dripping dozen.

I fished that summer too. It had been years, but this time I went with the Dexters and enjoyed it so much I decided to fetch my own tackle box and rod. I usually went after class, Tuesdays and Thursdays for a few hours before dinner. I fished a murky brown cove area; an offshoot of the Severn River, close to the Naval Academy. The Dexter boys showed it to me. It wasn't the best spot in the world to catch fish, but mostly I went to be by the water, to have my tiny ritual of tying line and hook, filling a cooler, baiting a worm, waiting. It was so quietly pleasurable to me. It still is. That little cove was in a private neighborhood, but the only people I ever saw fishing there were myself, the Dexters (sometimes), and the poorest oldest wisest black man I ever met, named Ezekiel Blanchard. Ezekiel Blanchard was unforgettable. He stayed at one end of the pier, I stayed at the other, the two of us going back and forth, hemming and hawing the whole time we fished. The more I came, the more I heard him speak, the more I came to believe he was the pier itself. He had a sound and look like none other.

"Eww boi, you gotcho self sumpin!

Mhmm, yeaaa you DO....

Good size too."

The first time I fished beside him, just us two on the pier, he put his rod down, came over and introduced himself, then walked back over to his rod to check his line while still talking.

"Now I know you new round here and all, my name Ezekiel by the way...but don't you be callin' me Zeke, now..."

"Dey always tryna call me Zeke," he continued.

"Who?" I asked.

"E'body since Ize 5 ye's ol'. Now I'm fiddy ye's olda den all um'. Don't see me tryna change none a dem names. I call dem names how it is! What chores?"

"Chores?" I asked.

"Name. What chore name?"

"Oh, Jonah."

"Jonah. Now das a good name. Haha! You en I got good names."

"Jonah, Jonah..." he kept repeating to himself under breath.

Each time I came back, I enjoyed Ezekiel's presence more and more. He was there to catch a catfish for dinner, he told me, and he almost always did. 'My wife, she goin' like dis one! Mhmm...' He was always there before me. When I'd get there, he'd be leaning against the rail, or sleeping in his fold out chair. Whenever he heard me arrive he'd put his things down and come over and shake my hand. 'Well helluh, my good friend.' he'd say. He wore the same outfit every time; big boxy blue jeans and a raggedy red flannel shirt, smeared with fish. When I'd leave I'd ask him how late he was planning on staying, and he'd say 'I be here all night, Jonah, All NIGHT!" Who knows if he left. Ezekiel Blanchard was like a great room of personality. A room that grew bigger and bigger the more you stepped inside of it. His mirth went out in all directions. It went out to himself, to me, to the fish below, and the whole dirty river we camped on. I hardly had to say anything to him. I would just listen to his stories, opinions, commentary on life. I could do that all day. So could he. But sometimes I know he got tired of hearing

YEAR OF PLENTY

himself and wanted to hear from me.

"You gotcho self a gurl?" he asked once.

"Not now I don't." I said.

"Well why not? Why don'tchu?"

"The girl I had is gone."

"Gone?!" he said, astonishingly.

"Yeah, she left me."

"Leftchu?! Whatchu do?!"

"Dumb things."

"Oh, mhmm." he nodded. "I understand...Be patient I say... .Was das gur's name anyhow?"

"Ellie."

"Ell-E? Did I say it right?"

"That's right."

"Ha-ha, das the whitest gurs name I eva heard!! Ell-E?! Hmmm, make me think of Eliahu. You know who da is?"

I shook my head.

"Das da book o' Job, Job's friend. Das Eliahu. You need to read dat! Come ova here, doh."

I put my rod down and came over. He leaned his rod against his thigh, still holding it, then pulled a tattered square of laminated paper out of his flannel shirt pocket.

"Read dat." he said.

I read it.

"No. Read dat out loud."

"Ecclesiastes 9." I read aloud:

"Read de whole thing."

"Enjoy life with the wife whom you love, all the days of your vain life that he has given you under the sun, because that is your portion in life and in your toil at which you toil under the sun."

31

"You see dat?" he said. "I read dat evy day. Das my wife. She my po'tion. She is…I tell you…she is. I ain't go messin' dat up now. No suh! Dat woman…Mmmm…I ain't got nobody lika in my whole life. Read dat evvy day. Tell you what, Iza chump, a bad, bad man way back den- prolly yo age! Ho-ho!! Yea… Butchu learn, you learn, you do…I prolly still ain't dat good, but betta. Betta. Yes suh! Das why my wife like it when I come out here. Says I get calm down. You find choself a gur like dat, you keepa. Yeah, you keepa, yes suh…"

I folded the paper and gave it back to him and he said

"Now check yo LINE boi! You prolly loss yo bait liss'n'me! Ho-ho!"

That summer and the start of fall, I came back to that cove as much for Ezekiel's presence than for any fish I could have caught. He was unhurried, unworried, and hopefully, in some way, that rubbed off on me.

Up until the start of fall classes, I lived in a kind of immature timelessness, disbelieving that time had any real hold on me, any real demand on my living. Life would just unfold, I needn't press it. Ellie would be there, my parents would be there, I would find my way without fuss, etc. And that wasn't true. Every day from then on proved that wasn't true. The days shortened. Full time classes started. Mom got depressed. I got depressed because Mom got depressed. Everything that happened in our family had a reverb. We felt what each other felt. Daddy told me he went on a date with a 29 yr old who "had real energy, a real level head about her." and I laughed. I thought 'What a relief. I think the 29 yr old is the only one with a level head right now.' So my family- we scattered into the season, having nothing substantial to hold on to, not even each other during that time. And hope? We had little; in Clara more than anyone. My days were flat footed; there was no fleetness in me; no flight. The going of my life, the intensity of it, was like an endless cool down. Fall and winter and spring, I entered into this pace of life and came to be ok with it. I did my classes half heartedly, but did them nonetheless. I never skipped. On weekends I hiked, read by the docks, got back into running. I missed Ellie terribly the whole time. I never heard from her. The thought of her usually came to me at the close of a day; after class, driving back home through the chilly sunset, and it filled me with longing such as I have never felt. I had no one to tell either. The 'missing her' was just there, living inside me, a feeling birthed in my heart, then spreading into all my capillaries and arteries, muscles and nerve endings. And as it spread it did not dilute, but became equally potent over every inch of me. That's longing. That was my longing. Was it cancerous? I don't know. But if it was, if I was dying, I was at least dying with a keen sense of having a real, beating heart still left within me.

That winter, Ellie came back home. She sent me a message on my phone that said 'Back in town. Want to catch up?' I couldn't believe it. I replied that I did, and we found a time to get dinner at a local pub. On the day of, I honestly didn't know how I felt about seeing her. I wanted to see her, but something unnerved me about the straightforwardness of her message to me, out of the blue. I held myself in check. More, I called my longing into doubt. I called it into doubt, because until I received that message, I didn't honestly believe that I would hear from her again. And yet that belief- that I wouldn't see her again- was what gave my longing its force, its fire. The dinner went well. It went fine. I was astonished to see her. She was the same and different. She was energetic, her hair was lighter, she had a little diamond stud in her nose. She was full of stories, too; all that she had been doing and involved in. She did most of the talking; she talked about this person and that person and this class she's taking next semester 'and like, Jonah, I think I'm really passionate about nonprofits now. I might apply for a State department fellowship next year in Hong Kong. I'm not sure, but I probably will.' While she spoke, there was a question seeping out of me that deafened me to so much of what she said: 'Where are you, Ellie? Where are you, the Ellie I know?' I must have been so plain and boring next to her. Especially when she asked me about myself; I had so little to say. I said that I've been keeping on, the usual. Classes aren't too bad, I've been hiking...Anyway, dinner was a blur. Afterward we stopped off at 7-11, got coffees, and sat talking in my car. We settled down. There was more space between our words. It was easier to listen. She was telling me about a party she got drunk at, and in the middle of her story, she stopped. I looked at her, and she let out a loud "Humph"

"What?" I asked.

She shook her head.

"What, Ellie?"

"Hearing myself...I got crooked, didn't I?"

I shrugged.

"Maybe you did, maybe you didn't. I don't know yet. You haven't finished your story."

"Ha, it doesn't get much better."

Then she did something I didn't see coming. She turned to

me and pulled down her lower lip, revealing her bottom teeth. She said,

"See that? I never had my Dad fix em'. See how they're crooked?"

"Uh huh, not too bad though. Why didn't you?"

"I like 'em' that way, now. But I liked 'em back when I was little too, for whatever reason. They've got character. They remind me that I'm human, that I've got some slant to me. There's always gonna be some parts of me that even a perfect set of braces can't fix or straighten out."

"Preach it." I said.

"You know what I mean."

"I guess you are getting crooked, aren't you?" I said.

"Probably." she laughed.

"But I do know what you mean. Look," I pointed to my nose. "You see?"

"Your nose?"

"Yes my nose! crooked as can be. Crooked now and crooked till the day I die. No, I get it. I know what crooked feels like. We've each got our stories. Feels like it's so close to you sometimes, so close to who you are, that you couldn't separate it from the person you want to be at the end of the day, even if you tried."

"Who do you want to be at the end of the day, Jonah?"

"Not the punk I am right now."

"I don't think you're a punk."

"Then you don't know me well enough. If I'm not a punk, I'm something close to it. At the end of the day...at the end of the day, I wish the good things would last longer than they did. I want to have work that matters; something to put my back and soul into, that wears me out good. Parents who stay together;

my sister live out her dream. Maybe I need to go on a road trip, or get in a fist fight- something…howl at the moon…something, if that's what it takes."

"If that's what it takes, for what?" she said.

"To come alive, I guess. Be woken up, or reminded of it somehow…It's not all bad. It's not. That's what I'm getting at, what I'm trying to understand myself. From the outside, I know my life seems bland. Even talking about it makes me feel that way. But you see, it stings me once in a while. Even before I met you, it would come to me in the boredom of the day: this bliss. This simple, uninvited bliss. I get it when I'm driving, too, sometimes, late at night; a sting. A sting of something good, that's all I can name it right now- it comes and goes…Lately it just seems to go. Anyway…"

When I finished talking, water had caught up imperceptibly in my eyes. I pulled a napkin from my pocket and dabbed them.

"I'm sorry, Ellie, for this. I'm sad as hell."

"Sad from what?"

I tossed my hands.

"From what I threw away. Overtalking just now. The whole curse of this year with no end in sight. Seeing you all changed. And me the same. And havin' no clue what to do next."

"Let yourself be sad, Jonah."

And I said "Why the hell would I want that?"

And she said "Cuz' you're feelin' something true for once, you're not fleein' the scene, or trying to be some brute who pushes through at all cost. You're figuring out the cost."

"Yeah," I said. "Or getting jipped!"

"And us," she said. "who knows…all I know is that you never said anything like that to me, ever. Not when I was with you."

"I've never said anything like that to anyone, any time."

"Why not?"

"Don't know."

"Why tonight, then?"

I looked up, into the great, green eyes. I said,

"Because you're here tonight."

"Jonah…"

"It's true. I know you gotta go soon. I'll miss you. Thank you for seeing me, though."

She reached over and gave me a hug, and after she left I sat there awhile in my car looking at my hands in my lap. I felt everything.

We reach that boundary line in our heart where we can't step any farther. We're not allowed. Not yet. I don't pray formally, but maybe that's the nearest I've ever been to real holiness; that lucid, post-tears peace. It was not a thing I did, per se. I didn't accomplish, or earn anything, not even the empathy of another. It wasn't how inspired we spoke in a moment of need, or even what we spoke; whatever chaos burst from our lips. But that we let ourselves be heard. We let. We let our voices voice their madness, and our hands ungrip the wheel, and fall into our empty laps. We let the girl walk away, only because it's right. And we don't know how it is, but it is. We were strong and weak. We let.

You would think that after my last conversation with Ellie, something would have changed; I would have smartened up, learned a lesson from my own words, or else dropped what I was doing and ran after her. But I was stubborn. I had the habit of resistance. I replayed our conversation in my head dozens of times, and the more I replayed it the more stupid I sounded.

Therefore, I closed myself to it. In time, I allowed the memory of that evening to dissipate, and be just a memory, one of many. A month or two after, I saw my daddy for the first time in four months. Neither of us were well, but him especially. He seemed depressed. He hadn't shaved. We hardly made eye contact that night. We met at a bar and sipped our beers drudgingly. We watched the screens. I played with a coaster at my fingertips. At one point he yawned, then asked,

"So what's new with that girl? What's her name...Ellen?"

"Ellie." I said.

"Yeah, her."

"She's at school."

"School, huh? You still with her?"

"No. I told you I wasn't. Long ago."

"You done with her?"

"For now, I guess."

He grinned darkly.

"You guess? You need to stop guessin'...You're beginning to sound too much like me; full o' non committals."

My blood rose. I had an urge. I wanted to tell him everything, right then and there, and quit our act, quit our misery. But all I mustered was a nod.

"We'll see." I said.

"See what?"

"See what happens, if anything." I said.

"With her?" he said.

"Uh huh."

He shook his head and made that grin again.

"Guess so. It's your life." he said, taking one big swallow of beer, "It all goes crooked eventually. You know that...look at...well, I don't need to go there..."

He lifted his almost finished glass of beer, I mine. We clinked over those parting words, drank down the whole thing, wiped our mouths, and left. I thought of that last cheers for a while. Or how it wasn't cheers at all; if it was, it was cheersing a forlorn fact in our lives; that we were lonely men. Men without women, men without each other, men without real words, men without anything daring in our lives. I thought of the word 'crooked', too. Daddy and Ellie both used that word last time I was with them, but they used it in totally different ways. Her 'crooked' confessed something; the crookedness of her own life. His merely admitted it; he meant it to mean the crookedness of the world at large, life in general. There's a world of difference between confessing and admitting, and I heard it that evening.

Pubs are supposed to make men feel like men. But I left that evening feeling less a man than I ever did before. I was miserable for my daddy, and miserable for myself, but if there was any goodness in our meeting, it was that I got to see him in the flesh. My mother asked how it went when I got back. I said 'Ok.'

"How's he doin'?" she asked.

"I really don't know, to be honest."

"Didn't you guys talk?"

"Yeah...but about nothing, really."

I was standing in the living room. As we talked, she scooted around me and straightened a few pillows on the couch. She cleared a glass from the coffee table, refolded a throw. My mother tidies when she's worried. I stayed in the living room while she went about her errands. I heard the faucet turn on in the kitchen, and for some reason when I heard that sound, I closed my eyes and wept all a sudden; a hot, quick flash of tears, just like before. Then I stanched my eyes with my shirt before she came back. Home. Home is hard, isn't it? I remember being at home in high school, when daddy would come back, angry and bitter. He'd be tired from work and he would treat us all like ragdolls, but my mother foremost. He looked at us with a grimace, like there was something wrong with us being there. We'd go silent, and he'd kind of follow us from room to room, storin' up some invective, anything that he could find to criticize, any discharge from his own foul heart. Sad thing is, I have no idea where that anger came from, none of us do, or who put it there to begin with. But it dominated the house. My sister and I would go up to our rooms where we would hear him pacing below. Pacing and pacing.

My affection for Ellie, all my thoughts of her, whatever I believed about our relationship, was trammeled under the foot of that last conversation with my daddy. Many more months went by in a sluggish state of existence, before I felt anything that felt like living. I craved normalcy. And I searched for it. Some time in the spring of my freshman year, I go to this party and meet a girl. We hit it off, and at the end of the night, go back to her place. Jess, I think her name was. We're in her room, (tiny little closet room, creaky twin bed) and she takes off this dress she wore. One that gives her more curves then she's got. She's soft looking, undressed. I chuckle a bit, laying there. I say "You look beautiful, I think." She looks at me, hearing that hesitation, and says "Is that what you think?" Then she goes, "You look handsome, I think." I taste my own poison in those words, but I don't stop smiling at her, else I won't get what I came for. Either way, she can't read my thoughts. The more I look at her face the more I see these little black clumps of mascara around her eyes, and my stomach just turns. It kills the humor. I stare at the ceiling. I went on with whatever we did, but like a puppet, because deep down I was dead. Plain dead. Not 'playin' dead.' Dead, dead. Dead as dead comes. I left early the next morning, and probably talked to that girl two more times ever, about class assignments.

After that, I didn't touch a girl for a while. Some of my buddies wondered if I was alright. Was I sick or gay, they wondered, since I didn't talk to girls, and since I said I didn't want to talk to them, either. Truth was: I was sick for one girl still, and I was sick to admit it, even to myself. Nothing sounded more foolish in my mind than my own honest desire. Sophomore year was upon me at the community college, and it promised to be as unambitious as it ever had. Everyone was thinking about the future. Future plans. Some wanted to transfer schools. I wasn't so worried. I was an accounting major and fairly certain I would have a job after school. My classmates were wracked though. We all sort of hated our lives for different reasons. But there were a few good things that happened that Fall that came unforeseen. First, time was time. Time tempered my parents' separation; it smoothed the animosity between them. They inquired of each other, through me, less out of bitterness, more out of well wishing, even nostalgia. Second (a big Second), my daddy had an accident, which I'll say more about later, that changed him, and us, and a whole trajectory of things. But the day before Halloween, he drove over unannounced and placed two pumpkins on our stoop. They sat next to a wagon from our childhood that my mother now used for decoration, filling it with hay and gourds and such- and he left a little note with the pumpkins that said

"Happy Halloween!

Carve something spooky!"

We could tell it was him by his handwriting. When I saw the note, I was shocked. Shocked to see that exclamation point and sense the jest. We hadn't heard him humored, or frivolous, in a long time. I wondered what gave. A week later my mother made a pumpkin pie and had me drop it off at his doorstep. He called her that night and said "Thank you." It was a short conversation, she said. Later , when we were getting ready for bed, I could hear her sobbing in her room. I knocked and came in. She was sitting up in bed with her hair a mess, her eyes red, and a tissue in her hand. When I came closer, she looked up at me, lips quivering, then turned her eyes and looked down. I didn't say anything. I just climbed in bed beside her, put my arm around her, and she trembled against me. Cried and cried. That Fall, Clara came home more often, too. She had met her fair share of show biz rejection in New York City. and I think home was good for her. She liked being back by the water again, being by the Bay. She missed it. It was a welcome change from the city, and I think it was the first time in a long time when Clara felt truly at home, and not preoccupied with something else, or somewhere else. I saw my mother and sister the most; there was an uncommon ease between us, a lightness of being that I couldn't quite pinpoint, but that I believed had begun with my father, with those pumpkins note. I wanted to know what happened. Before I called him, he called me. He said he wanted to see me, so we met for lunch, days after, at a local sandwich shop. He arrived before me, and when I saw him I could tell that there was something different. His right arm was in a sling. His face was warm, smiling. When he saw me he brightened up, came over and embraced me with his good arm.

"What happened to you?!" I asked.

"Order first, then I'll explain."

When we had our sandwiches I said,

"So…?"

"So….I was mugged."

"Mugged?! What! When?"

"Bout a week and a half ago. Here's how it went…I was taking a woman out in Baltimore, we were finished dinner and I was walking her back to her place- it's not even late at this point, 930, 10, and I hear two guys should behind us and I look back to see who it is and there's these two kids like your age- a white guy and a black guy, baggy clothes on both of em', and when I turn, they start callin' us names. But we keep walking, thinking they'll leave us alone. I've been around guys like that before, and they haven't done anything, they're all talk…And mind you, there's still cars out at this point, there's still people out, it's not like we're totally alone. Then one of them says,

"Ay yo, turn nat bitch around…Come ere…Stop walkin'…You hear me?!…Turn nat bitch around."

We ignored them and kept walking, but I tell you, my blood was beginning to boil. Then it seemed like they fell away or left. I dropped the lady off, apologized for those guys. She said 'It's Baltimore, unfortunately. It happens.' Anyway, I start leaving and when I turn the block back the way I came, I see the two kids standing a street over, and when they saw me they started coming for me. They weren't saying anything so I didn't think they were actually going to do anything. But they were walking aggressive, getting closer and I said 'Fuck off! I'll call the police' The white guy laughed and said 'Dey ain't gon do nuffin.' So I took out my phone to call the police when the black kid sprints and tackles me from behind, and the other guy punches me in the stomach and mouth and all the air comes out of me. Then the white guy kicks me on the back of the head, three times maybe, like hard, really hard. And I'm just there on the sidewalk, my face to the ground, right beside a parked car, and I can see another car passing on the road from underneath. Then one of them picks me up from the back and shoves me forward onto my face. That's how I got this scrape across my cheek. He does it again and again, just shovin' me. I got no fight in me. I can't move. I'm barely conscious, dizzy from the head blows. Just my eyes and ears are functioning, feels like. I feel one of them reach around my pants for my wallet, which he takes. Takes my phone too. From that vantage point I could only see their shoes-big colorful reflective basketball shoes. The black guy comes around to face me and crouches down and flashes a blade in front of my eyes. 'Speak one mo' word and I cutcho mouff open. Dontchu bring dat bitch round here eva. Eva!' Then he cradled the back of my head and smushed my face onto the sidewalk. At this point I was losing it, but I could still hear them talking behind me. The white guy says 'Whatchu do? You cut im? and his friend replies 'He ain't even wurf it. Look at im. He ain't even wurf it. He gon die soon anyway.'

Daddy paused from the story and took a few bites from his sandwich. When he continued there was a different tone to his voice; an urgency he'd never used before.

"Anyway, when I was face first on the ground, and they had left, and I was probably moments from passing out, I couldn't stop thinking about what they said; how they didn't want to waste their blade on me, that I would be done soon anyway. What crossed my mind, then, wasn't those thugs, not even the pain I felt in my arm or face. I thought of you guys. Thought of myself. Thought how one second I'm hummin' along, the next I'm seconds away from being gone for good. Tell you what, I regret a lot, Jonah."

"Yeah," I said, "but what about those guys!? Did you ever call the police? You need to!"

He shook his head.

"It's not the guys, honestly. That's not what killed me in the situation. There's always gonna be men- I should say kids-like that, because that's what they know, that's all they've ever known. Is scarin' the people that cross their block. I'm not saying that they're innocent, or shouldn't get in trouble, or that I wouldn't want to kick them to pieces if I had the chance..."

"What are you saying then?"

"I'm saying I want more for us," he said, gesturing with his good hand. "More for you and I and our family. It's amazing that I'm alive. I hesitate to say it, but that incident may have been the best and worst thing that's happened to me in years."

"Getting mugged?!"

"Getting mugged, and feeling my life at its edge. How completely breakable and disposable I was...I am! Feeling authentic peril, and authentic dissatisfaction in my own wasted time. Most of all, these past years. I've been going head over heels for my own death."

I wanted to ask him what happened, how he got back, why he didn't call us immediately...but he said,

"Now, hold up Jonah, hold up. I got a question for you now."

"What is it?"

"Do you love that girl?"

"Who? Ellie?"

"The one from a while back…yeah, Ellie."

"Ellie, I don't know." Just saying her name made all those thoughts come rushing back.

"No, really, do you?"

"Yeah…sure. No, I do. I do."

"Sure? Sure you love her?"

I nodded.

"Don't say it like that, then. Let's talk straight for once. You still see her?"

"Not lately."

"You want to though?"

"I would."

"Cut the crap - just say yes."

"Yes, then."

"You kissed her yet?"

"Sort of."

"What do you mean?"

"I mean sort of, a long time ago."

He shook his head.

"I'm not asking if you've fooled around with her. I'm asking if you've kissed her. They're different."

"Of course."

"Of course?"

"Yes! Why do you keep asking like that? I'm almost 22 years old, you think I haven't kissed a girl?!"

"Not just that. Do you know how to kiss a girl?"

"Yeah, I do. Why, you think I don't? Why are you asking me this stuff, anyway?"

"I know you don't…I know you never seen it from me, or learned it from me. Heck, I never learned it from my own father, and that's a crying shame. I wish I would have kissed your mother better. Talk all you want about love and security and fulfillment in life - those are big broad strokes and ideas…But love is built by inches, maybe even centimeters. All those gestures add up. They become something." He knocked his knuckles on the table and looked off, sad and reminiscent looking. "Yeah," he said, making an inch with his pointer finger and thumb "inches. No one ever told me that. I never told you, my father never told me. But I believe it now, and figured I'd better tell you, now or never."

"What's that got to do with…?"

"Everything!" He jumped in and said, "Look at this sling! I'm a broken bird. I coulda been dead!" He held that last phrase in his mouth as if it were so real to him, like he could taste it."Look at me." he said.

"I am."

"Take hold of what matters most. Take hold of it now. Don't postpone. Look at me! Look at me! Look at the past few years. It's all postponing! I don't brag about it either. I've made so many mistakes I could literally fall into a depression on the spot if I thought about it too long. But forget that for right now. Take hold of what matters. Take hold of that girl. Start small. Learn how to kiss a girl. Learn how to kiss YOUR girl."

"She's not mine."

"Quit saying stuff like that!"

"It's true."

"I don't care if it's true. It's not true! You said you loved her, right?"

"Yeah."

"Then learn how to kiss her. Learn how to speak kind to her."

I laughed. I had never seen him in that mood before; speaking so earnestly, impassioned, and still somewhat angry."

"How am I supposed to do that?" I asked.

"Kiss? You want to know how to kiss? Lord...Haha...That's a question, right there...You watch someone do it well. Don't be a creep, but watch. Watch. Don't be afraid to watch. Let me tell you something: there's an elderly couple at the local McDonald's who comes in every morning after church, wearing the same outfit almost everyday- it's funny. I can tell they come from church because she takes their daily missal to the table and sits down while he goes and orders food. When he comes back, he takes her hand, they say grace, and right after that he leans over and kisses her on the cheek. But he doesn't *just* kiss her. He doesn't kiss her fast or sloppy. He takes his time. And it's not because he's old. It's because he knows it matters! After he kisses her he seems to look at the spot on her face where he just kissed her- he admires it! He keeps his eyes fixed on that spot for a moment, with great wonder and affection, as if that little gesture left a greater mark than he would ever live to see. He does that every morning I'm in there, without fail....You see? One kiss; well planned, well timed, well meant...you could write a novel on, you could change the world with...or at least your own world. That's what I mean by kissing well."

"Here's the other thing," he said. "It's not the technique. Anyone can learn technique. All you kids care about is technique. Anyone who can't handle mystery- or I should say - anyone who can't STOMACH mystery, loves technique. They want everything simple, quick, easily learned, easily applied, critical thinking, yadda yadda. We miss so much. The best things in this world are moved by more than just efficiency. More than just learning How. Way more! Love is the key. It sounds so feeble to say that out loud, but that's all I know. Haven't practiced it much myself, but that's what I know. Learn how to love, and kissing will come. And sometimes the opposite…But believe me, it'll come."

Where will weight come from? Where will we hear the words that send us back on our asses with a blow of wisdom? And from whom? My father acquired anger in the time he left my mother. Anger that was bad, and anger that was good, too; a good, hold nothing back sort of anger that sometimes speaks directly to fools, breaks through our timidity. Before then, he lived passively, suffered passively and it bred passivity the more. It bred bitterness too. When I left lunch that day, I knew he would not let me do the same. That same afternoon I called Ellie. It was November. It had been a year since last we talked; a year of nothing, a year of wanting, a year of feeling stymied, a year of being dislocated from the core of who I was. When I called her, my heart was beating, beating. Fast fast fast. I paced in my room as I waited for her to pick up, and when she said 'Hello?' my voice cracked.

"Hi, Ellie!" That's when my voice cracked.

"Hi Jonah."

"Hi, Ellie…I was thinking of you earlier, and…wondering, are you going to be back this summer?"

"Yeah, I'll be back for a while. I'm graduating, you know?"

"Yeah, I know."

"Well, yeah, let's get together when I'm back. It'll be good to see you."

"You too. Ok…bye."

My heart was still thumping. It did not abate. It thumped in fits, day and night. I can't believe I called her. I can't believe we spoke. That night I drove. I packed my unbelief and drove across the windy bridge by the Naval Academy, parked by the water, rolled the windows down, and let in a flood of warm whipping air. I was at home. The air was moaning, the water was rough, my heart was full. No time passed. None. Hardly. The following week crawled by. I slept on the floor every night that week, unable to sleep on the bed. I thought too much. I ate too little. I kept telling myself I thought too much, which made me think more. I forgot to drink enough water, so I woke every morning with a killer headache. I thought the headache was because of the heartache. I was one big ache. I hated it, but I couldn't stop it. I abided in it. More like, I was at the mercy of it, even ashamed of it because I thought 'This is not normal. this is not what normal people are like.' But now I know that's not true. They are. Additionally, I planned many things that I wanted to say to Ellie when I saw her. Dinner would be nice, I thought. That would be our plan. But that's not what happened. She called me and said 'Jonah, what if we go on a morning run again?' Morning run, I thought to myself. 'That'd be nice.' I said. 'I haven't run in a long time, though' 'Me too.' she said. 'Ok, I'm game.' I said. 'Me too.' she said.

That morning we ran. We ran. We ran. I want to keep writing that. We didn't say much. We were both, perhaps, slightly breathless for many words. But there was reticence too. It was good to be on the move; picking up an old habit along an old route. It was lovely running past remembered houses and yards, with Ellie beside me, like before. At one point I slowed and let her overtake me, and got a good look at her. Seeing the swishing hair from behind, the bright shoes- she loved bright shoes, chartreuse especially- the soft morning light, it all had a deep effect on me. I missed her, I missed her so much, more than I knew. When we were close to the finish she looked behind at me, raised her brows and said,

"See who wins…" and took off, and then me. I got as close as her heel in a sprint, but she was too fast that day and I said to her, heaving at the end,

"How'd you get that fast?" and she said,

"I didn't lose it all, Jonah! Still got some kick, thank you!"

After running, we went home separately to see our families, and decided to meet up later for dinner.

At dinner I got deja vu. I got it as soon as they started bringing out the bread and butter.

"Ellie, I got deja vu." I said.

"From what?"

"Just now, being here."

"You think it's deja vu?"

"Why, you feel it too?"

"Not that, not deja vu, but something similar."

"What would you say it is?"

She thought about it.

"It's sneaking nostalgia."

"Sneaking nostalgia?"

"Yeah, something about this feels sneaky."

"But nostalgia? Nostalgia for what?"

"Jonah, come on. We went to dinner here before. Look, see that guy, the bartender. Remember him?"

"I do. Same guy. Yeah, we did go here pretty often, didn't we?"

"Yeah," she said. "You don't have to use my phrase though. It doesn't have to be sneakingly nostalgic to you."

"No, it is, it is. I am nostalgic, but it's less the place. It's less about us being *here*..."

I paused, arriving at my own words gradually

"Less about here, and more about who, *who* we're here with."

I paused again. The waiter came. Ellie was picking her bread apart into smaller and smaller pieces on her plate. When the waiter left I started again,

"I'm nostalgic that you're here. I know that much. I can't avoid saying that, or saying it so forthright. I'm nostalgic because I'm surprised, first, that I called you, and second, that you picked up, and third, that you said yes to seeing me, and fourth, that you're here with me. Goodness, it's been a year? More? You can't plan this, can you, looking back?. Now we're back at our old spot and somehow everything is different, and everything the same, and this entire day has been like playing a favorite song of mine- one I haven't heard in a long time- at least for me it has. I guess I'm just happy that I'm here. Here with you."

"I'm surprised too," she said. "I shook a little when I got your call because I didn't expect it, and honestly, I was thinking about not coming back here for a while. It's not that I had something somewhere else...it's...it's you, like you said. I thought of you, a lot. More than I wanted, more than I'd like to admit, more than was good for me, probably. I didn't want to be back in this town, Glen Burnie, even though there is something small town or suburb in me I can't get away from. That kind of makes me cringe just saying it, but it's true. I've always had a disdain for this place, don't know if I ever told you that, let alone being with a guy from this place. I looked down at hometown romances, ever since I was small; Glen Burnie high school sweethearts. I was turned off by the simple folks who stayed put and settled down and worked average jobs and never saw anything else.

What did they live for, I thought. I honestly thought that. And I did, and I do, want real love. Romance, you know. I never made much of it in high school, but every girl's got that desire somewhere- either hiding within her, or else she flaunts it head to toe, so everybody sees. Lots of times it's both; the hiding and the flaunting. The daydreams…There's so much to people. Don't ever think that the flaunting girls, the easy girls as they call them, are actually easy. Nobody's easy, no matter how much they throw themselves around. They've got depths that not even they have seen. Likewise, don't think that all the hidden girls are closed, severe and high standards, like their meek eyes and tight lips might suggest. Their fortresses can crumble at a glance, just like everybody else, just like their mothers and grandmothers and great grandmothers did, from the foundations of the world. All great romance is a stretch. And stretching is painful. It's the painful necessity. Like in running. You know that. It's not just preventative, though we always speak about it that way. As if we only ever ran or gave our hearts or went through life, avoiding risks, avoiding the fall. It's more than preventative; it's strengthening. It's loosening. It loosens our hard selves. It enables us to run free, free without constantly fearing injury, or wondering if we're going to all of a sudden break like china. But anyway, back to was I saying earlier, I thought that real love had high stakes - and it does, I know that, but I believed the movies, all of them, and those stories of lovers during the war, or when one of them has cancer or they're going through some horrifying injustice, and their love is lived at the highest pitch, and I was always waiting for something like that to seize me. I am still waiting for that, for an epic to be a part of- because most of the time I feel like a bore. I feel petty. What I saw growing up was my parents and their marriage. That was my image of

YEAR OF PLENTY

lasting love. Lasting love as far as I observed was tedious and uncelebrated. My dad cleans teeth. My mom cleans the house. Lots of cleaning. Love was a miscellany of to-dos and leftovers, bagging leaves on the weekends, complaints and coping with complainers. They'd peck each other on the cheek before bed, but that was it. And college has been all that too, in a way. It was a different kind of romance, though; it was all BIG; it was all YOU; big dreams, big plans, go abroad, know what you're doing, stay connected, stay busy, plans, plans, plans, always next, always the after party. Never just the party. Never just good friends. Always grad school, you know? Always advancement. No one told me why. Seriously, from the beginning. Why I was thrust into motion so early and told to keep spinning. No one said. Not my parents, not my school, not the people I call friends. I assumed growth was motion, and anything less, was less than living. But can I not grow and be still? That's what I wonder."

In the time she spoke, our food came and was getting cold now. We both ordered steak. We took a few bites, and she continued.

"Over time, I built up resistance to this place; for all the reasons I just said. It wasn't dislike, so much as restlessness. I never showed it much either. I kept it to myself. I would have thrown them all to the wind, too, if it weren't for you. You were the last stubborn piece in all this. Yes, you. You were after me, Jonah. You were so immature back then…and you weren't even epic or romantic. You had the same long hair as you do right now, and sometimes, I'm not even sure if you wanted to come after me. Sometimes it seemed like you didn't; like you disliked me- or you disliked how much you liked me. Remember? Because none of your friends acted the same way toward any girl, and I knew you wanted to be liked by them. I knew you wanted something to show, or prove to them, and probably to yourself...but you kept coming. Whether willful, or will-less, you did. Something overshadowed you. I could see it. Time went by, and Good Lord! YOU CUT MY HAIR!- that's another story! But you did! You were mad, You ARE mad..." She coughed-laughed-sobbed. Why are you so mad? Why did you come after me? You were the only guy who really came after me, who was interested in awkward, quiet, track running Ellie; Ellie who would go to her room and eat mac and cheese by herself and watches cartoons still. I still watch cartoons, Jonah! Do you know that? Why did you come after me?"

"Because I liked you. And every time I saw you or got near you, I wanted to get your attention and talk to you. I like talking to you. I did back then and I still do. I missed talking to you when you weren't here. I'd rather be talking to you than doing most anything."

"You mean that?"

"Yeah, it's true."

"Except fishing..." she said.

"Maybe even that."

"What happened though?"

"What happened when?"

"Before I left, it seemed like you left. Left yourself. Like you just walked away from life. Your body was still here but you were gone somewhere."

I nodded, though it was so painful to think of that time.

"I did leave. You're right. I was so scared. Scared of everything. Ashamed too. Ashamed of who I was, ashamed I couldn't get into a real school like the rest of you, and didn't even try to. Ashamed of my family, ashamed I couldn't go after you. Or I felt I shouldn't keep trying to go after you, since my life was at a standstill, and you had some momentum at least. Plus, I knew I hadn't treated you well either, before you left. I was a man I didn't know. Not even a man. A body, and a will, and a ghost, all moving in different directions. It was like there was a big hand clamped over the back of my neck, holding it down, not allowing me to look up and see what was out there, but keep me staring at my two dumb feet."

"I don't think they're dumb." she said.

"You're bout' the only one…"

"Well they brought you here, didn't they?"

"They did."

"That's something."

"That is something. Something I'm quite in awe of, actually."

"I thought of you a lot, Jonah. You know that, right?"

"I honestly never thought you did."

"Why?"

"Because you were away."

"Away?" she scoffed. "Away is nothing. You can't flee your own heart and mind. You can drown things out- and I did- but they come back, they surface. You can distract them for a while, be around people 24 hours a day, put in the earbuds, busy yourself with events, jump off the deep end, all that stuff. But those thoughts remain, They grow, even. Eventually it's exhausting to keep distracting yourself from that tiny little voice that wants to speak its piece. Jonah…I thought of you. Trust me. Almost every day. In my dorm room, and on my way to class. In the middle of parties. I'd be in the middle of a party, somewhere, usually an ugly frat basement with people handing me drinks and calling my name. Other people screaming lyrics, and some idiot with his arm on my shoulder…and of all the thoughts or scenes that cross my mind, right then and there; it was that time we went to that stupid barn party and had a terrible time. And how I wished I'd rather be there than here…Know why? Because you were there. Yeah, I thought of that once."

"I thought you never did." I said.

"Oh come on! Come on…we all think of ourselves as the fool; the one who can't stand up straight anymore, the one who's every stray thought goes to that one person over and over. We're all the person who doesn't pray, or want to pray, but finds it somehow in their capacity to pray when they think of that one person…oh yes…We're all like that. We've all got our madness tucked away, thinking no one knows, hoping no one knows the real extent of it. We're way madder than the words we use. We're all in love with the boy from home, who cut our hair while we were sleeping- and we don't know why we are, or how it adds up, but even if we did know how or why, it wouldn't change a thing. We're in love. We love that boy."

"Love?" I repeated to myself.

"You knew I did that?" I covered my eyes with my hands. I groaned. "Ellie, why are you still here? I'm serious this time." I said.

"I just told you. You don't believe me?"

"It's hard to believe. You don't want to leave?"

She shook her head.

"Who are you?!" I said.

Ellie had a way of answering without words; with a single, all encompassing look that said everything she needed to say, and sometimes more. That was the look she spoke to me across the table. Then she reached down and fidgeted with something under the table.

"What are you doing?" I asked.

"Wait. Here…" and she pulled up her shoe, a suede brown ankle boot, and gave it to me.

"What's this for?"

She laughed.

"It's my shoe!"

"I know it's your shoe. Why are you giving it to me?"

"To tell you I'm not going anywhere. After all, how could I without my shoe? So you better hide it from me before I second guess myself and take it back!"

At this point in the evening, with the scene set as it was, and if it happened to be observed by some curious onlooker: the restaurant, the table where we sat, the place setting, the half eaten food- none of that, none of the outward signs (save the woman's shoe in my possession) would have given a fair approximation of the beauty and aura and overwhelming feeling (tremendum) of that conversation. I was not on the ground. Jonah was levitating. My whole person was aswim with Ellie. I was so in awe of her; at that moment more than any time before. We laughed and laughed. The evening evolved by laugher. When we had spoken all that we could speak, we laughed. I put the boot on the table and she laughed, of course, and we talked about nothing, as she continued to nibble on the finely picked appetizer bread. I saw her then, as close to who she was, as who she really was…who she is. I knew that Ellie Beards was free like no other woman I ever knew- whatever made her free, and whatever made her a woman- she was both. Both were eternally important. Was it her hair? her voice? her makeup? her sex? her personality? All of that was part of it, but not the whole. How do I put it? It was like she had this one great invisible 'YES' welling up within her- a 'YES' I couldn't repeat (only she could), but only hope to know more of, descend deeper into, participate in. Whoever she was, I wanted a place in her. I wanted to be lost in her beautiful, undying, primitive, endless-as-the-ocean 'YES'."

After the bill I said,

"I've got two things for you, Ellie. One for today, and one for tomorrow, and that's just the beginning. The first we've got to drive to."

So we left the restaurant and I piggybacked her to the car.

"Where are we going?" she asked.

"You'll know," I said. When we got close she said,

"Oh, it's our old place! Our old 7-11...I haven't been here in awhile."

"Probably the last time you saw me." I said.

"Probably."

When I parked I said,

"Ellie-elms, I've got to tell you something. A secret... Something I haven't told anybody. Well, when I'm alone, by myself, thinking my own thoughts, and when I drill down into my little old soul...I see this place. I see this scene."

"This place? 7-11? haha"

"Yeah, this place. I don't know if it's this 7-11 exactly, but yes. I'm not kidding; a convenience store parking lot- I always see the scene in the middle of the night, when the store is glowing in an eerie huddle of light on a dark suburban street like this. The parking lot has worn out lines, black gum flattened on the curb, oil stains, there's a foreigner behind the register...Can you see it?"

59

"I'm seeing it right now."

"To me, it's the place where I go back to the most- this half-haunted place, a strange oasis on an empty street, a place where I've laid up so much regret."

"What from?"

I didn't have to say, I just looked at her.

"With me, you mean?"

"Yeah."

"Jonah..."

When she said my name like that, with that soft petition, I struggled to keep speaking, but I did.

"This afternoon, I thought this could be new. We could pick a new spot, not go back here like we usually did, when we'd come here and just worry about our lives."

"Except at the beginning..."

"Yeah, except at the beginning...but I don't just want to avoid hard moments or hard memories. I don't just want us to go back to the beginning. A lot of life has happened that's made us better for it. I've wanted to come here with you and know this spot differently, know it different than the past. Maybe even better, this time forth."

We were parked on the side of the store. I unbuckled in my seat and looked at her. She had this scouring face; a firm expression; part frown, part humored, part interested in what was coming.

"What are you doing?" she said.

I moved in closer.

"Ellie Marie Beards, I've never done this well...But, may I kiss you?

She waited and waited, and I saw her eyes skimming my face and she said,

"Yes."

I moved closer to her. Humorously, she put her arm rest down to block me, and laughed at the attempt, but I pushed it back up, and as I got closer her laughter subsided. In the last half second before my lips met hers, her eyes shut, then mine shut, and she let out this last bright, almost nervous breath of giggle, which I felt against my own lips. Then I kissed her. I tasted her lips, her tongue, lipstick. I smelled her skin, felt the shape of our faces opposed, my bent nose against her button nose. Then, wordlessly, we came apart, looked at each other for a moment, suspended, and then, just as wordlessly, our eyes closed and we drifted back, finding the face, lips, smell. Someone knocked on the window while we did. Neither of us saw. Neither of us cared. It was perfect.. Finally, we came apart and I kissed her on the forehead and went over to my side. I buckled up, started the car, and drove her home. On the way home I looked over and she had this complete, unrestrained grin on her face. She was staring out the window. And she was sitting sort of slumped, her hands not neatly in her lap but hanging wherever, and yes, still only one shoe on. When we got to her house I reached down and held up the shoe she gave me but she shook her head and said 'Keep it.' and left, and no words were needed after that. I took my time on that drive back home- full stop at every stop sign; everything slow, accelerating and decelerating; gradual. Gradually finding home.

The next day I picked her up in the afternoon, and we both had the same leftover smile stuck on our face from the night before. I felt like a boy. She looked like a girl. The world was a dream.

"Where are we going?" she asked.

"You always want to know, don't you?"

YEAR OF PLENTY

"Yes, I do."

"You'll know." I said.

Ten minutes later we pulled into the only barber shop in Glen Burnie I had ever been to. It had been years.

"Jonah! No!"

"Oh yes. Yes yes yes!"

"But you love your hair!"

"No I don't! I've wanted to cut it for a long time."

"Why didn't you?"

"Not the right time."

"Now is?"

"Yep. It's been ready."

"Why's that?"

"You already know. But I'll tell you more: three days before I decided to call you I almost chopped it all off with a shard of broken beer glass. But that would've looked terrible."

"You wanna get rid of it that bad, huh?"

"Yeah. That's why I'm glad you're coming with. I can make sure they don't butcher it!"

There was no one in the barber shop when we came in. The vietnamese barber took me right away and Ellie sat up front sucking on a dum-dum and reading men's magazines. I kept looking over at her; sitting cute and cross legged, enjoying her lollipop and flipping carelessly through the magazines. What a girl. What a good day I thought. After the barber spritzed my hair he asked what I wanted, and I heard Ellie smack the magazine down on the seat beside her and yell 'Butcher! haha' The barber looked over at her, and she said 'Butcher away!' I laughed, and he looked at me, confused, and I said 'What she said…go as short as you can.'

62

When the cut was done I was a new man, and I felt as naked as can be. I hardly recognized myself. Ellie said I looked like an ant, but that I still looked cute. Every couple of minutes she ran her hands over my prickly head. What a day, I thought. We went back to my house after. Ellie sat on the couch looking through family photo albums. I sat in the next room over, writing a letter to my daddy. The idea came to me last night, on my drive back home.

"What are you writing him about?" Ellie asked.

"That's a secret."

"As long as it's not about me."

The letter went like this:

Dear Daddy,

I haven't written you many letters before, certainly not one like this. I imagine when you read it, it will sound like I tore it out from my private journal and sent it along for sheer embarrassment. But no matter. It is what it is. I wanted to write you to tell you that I kissed the girl that I love, and that I haven't been the same since. I figured you should be the first to know. You inspired me, after all. I can't stop thinking about it. After dinner last night we went to that 7-11 across from the grocery on rte. 2. We were parked in the car, and I said Ellie Marie Beards, may I kiss you? I don't think I'd ever used her full name like that, and I doubt she'd ever heard me use her full name like that. Regardless, it sounded uncanny, but good, coming out of my mouth. I don't know what provoked me to say it like that. I knew I wanted to kiss her, maybe that was it. Other times I just went for it, and I we know how those went...She said yes, by the way. As I was coming over, she put down her arm rest, teasin' me, we both laughed at that. We were both nervous, I think, but me more than her, I know. She's always steady. Daddy, this girl- even after all this time, ups and downs, coming together, coming apart- she's like still water. I can't get over it. Anyhow, I put the armrest down, I move slowly toward her, she remains, and finally closes her eyes, waiting for me. Well, I go. We went to the left, not right. Slow, achingly slow. I could smell her before I could taste her. It was one long motion without any abruptness. No staccato. But interludes, yes. Pauses, yes. Silence, yes. The sound of our breathing, I remember. I don't want to forget it. At one point, our foreheads came together, and rested against one another. As if we shared a common weariness. I put my hand on the back of her neck, then brought her head forward and kissed her again. I'm no a poet, but I can remember a place, and sometimes a mood. She was wearing a white blouse, one of her shoes was off (another story!), in the backseat was a pile of textbooks from last semester. Also, someone knocked on our window while we kissed. We never saw who...

Those textbooks. When I saw them afterwards, I laughed. I thought of the knowledge in books, and how they shrivel in comparison to the wisdom of kiss- well, THAT kiss, especially. I know a kiss may be cheapened like all other things; debased, smeared, etc...but it need not be. Not all the debasing in the world, not all its wrong use (I would know...) can blunt its beauty. A kiss is fire. It's a perfect, dangerous act. It clears and fogs (smokes?), you know what I mean? I mean that when I kissed Ellie, I was lost and could not see. I could not think of anything or anyone else. A million trifling things went out the window. She was it! That's what I'm saying. Everything reduced, down to its simplest form, and what I was left with in my heart was one refrain: 'I love her, I love her, I love her'

I can't believe I'm writing you this letter! Guys don't write letters like this to their fathers. I know. That's why I'm writing it. Bear with me.

I mentioned trifles; it's funny how so many thoughts never came to me- plans for the future, plans with her even; fears, bad memories- all that seemed small. Suffering's the same way. People say that when they lose someone they love, so many things fall away- job, money, mortgage, retirement- all those things are straw. You know this. What I'm trying to articulate is that joy, love (whatever it is I share with Ellie) casts a similar spell, and that I am under it. A kiss isn't currency, I know that much. It shouldn't be. Pray I never treat it like it is. Hours removed, I can't stop thinking of it. I hope I don't either. It may be as important for me to remember THAT moment as it is for me to recall my birthday each year. That night, I don't remember when we stopped, just that we did. There was nothing more to do then but sleep and dream. I slept on my actual bed last night. Not the floor like I've been! Things are softer now.

You must be wondering how all of this came about? Do you remember your advice to me? You said 'Watch', and I did.

It was you. You! You won't believe me, but it was. When we left lunch that day, I thought of the only kiss I'd ever seen that stopped me in my tracks. I was 6 and Clara was 7. We had just come back from my soccer game, and I was still in my uniform,

YEAR OF PLENTY

cleats and all. You and mommy were getting ready for some party or whatnot that evening. I remember I was calling for mommy, clopping through the house, looking for her, and came finally to your bedroom, where the door to the bathroom was open and the light was on. I heard Clara and mommy talking, and I was quiet because my cleats were on the rug. I felt sneaky because I could see them in the bathroom getting ready, but they couldn't see me. Clara was looking up at mommy, who was fixing herself in the mirror, and looking so pretty. I couldn't see everything, though, because the door was half shut, but I snuck closer. I was going to spook them, but right as I was, you came from behind the door- you were in the bathroom, too. Getting ready, I suppose. You came right up behind mommy and kissed her once on the neck, then again, and she smiled and turned around- and little Clara, who looked scorned and scandalized all at once, and who was waiting to hand mommy her necklace- clutched mommy's leg and looked up at the two of you kissing. I'm not sure we knew what was going on, but I couldn't stop watching either. The two of us. You kissed mommy back, until she leaned against the countertop, and I think my mouth fell open. Clara! I saw her looking up at you two- completely moonstruck- we both were...I couldn't even really see your face because it was covered by mommy's red hair. Then, I'll never forget this: you held her head in your hands, very gently, right at her temples, and kissed her forehead. Then you went without a word back to what you were doing and left mommy and Clara alone there, and mommy turned and looked down at Clara staring up at her and flashed her a look with big eyes and a big smile. I received that look from where I stood, too.

So that's what I followed, I guess. That kiss. I remembered

66

it perfectly. Look at me; I sat down here to write you a short, straight-forward something, and it's taken the long windy route instead. I hope you'll see the best in this...All I know is that a kiss is more than a kiss, and now you know I know it! You led the charge. Don't let up, daddy. These days it feels I'm living in a year of plenty, and so, I hope are you...

As I was scribbling out the final words and salutation,
    "...Love you lots!

Sincerely,"

Ellie called me from the other room.
    "Oh Jonah, come here! Look how little you were."
    I left the letter unsigned and sat down next to the girl I love (I love! I love!), and she asked me 'What year was that taken?'

In the picture, my sister and I are 2 or 3, playing in the surf, while my father and mother lounge in the sand, looking out to sea.

"It was a year of plenty." I said. "Plenty of good; plenty to come."
    "Yes." she said. "It looks like it was."

At that, I finished the story. I was pleased with where it ended. I put the pencil down. I neatened the pages on my desk, and folded the one separate sheet into the size of a high school love note and placed it in my pocket. In the other room I heard a host of voices; my mother's, two children, and a woman's I knew so well. At their chatter, I remembered my errand from before, and it struck me then as the most important thing in the world. I climbed the stairs again to the stuffy attic; I sealed the box, pushing it toward the others, and descended that day with a squeaky wheeled reg wagon- just in time for pumpkin season.

Made in the USA
Columbia, SC
20 February 2023